BITE THE ICE
LAKESHORE U

BITE THE ICE

A LAKESHORE U PREQUEL STORY

L A COTTON

Go Lakes!
L.A.Cotton
-x-

Published by Delesty Books

BITE THE ICE
Copyright © L. A. Cotton 2022
All rights reserved.

This book is a work of fiction. Names, characters, places, and events are the product of the author's imagination or used in a fictitious manner. Any resemblance to actual persons or events is purely coincidental.

No part of this book may be reproduced or used in any manner without the written permission of the publisher, except by a reviewer who may quote brief passages for review purposes only.

Edited by Kate Newman
Proofread by Sisters Get Lit.erary Author Services

LAKESHORE U

Bite the Ice
A Lakeshore U Prequel Story

Ice Burn

BITE THE ICE

When Ella Henshaw agrees to attend the annual Bite the Ice party at Laker House with her best friend, she knows it's a bad idea. Especially, since it's a hockey party and she swore off hockey players a long time ago.

Enter Connor Morgan.

Handsome. Confident. With enough persistence to wear down even the most stubborn heart, he's determined to win over the girl he hurt in freshman year.

When he finds Ella at his team's annual Halloween party, it's his opportunity to finally make his move.

He's the hockey player who broke her heart. She's the girl he let slip through his fingers.

But can Connor persuade Ella to give him one more chance?
Or will she always be his biggest regret?

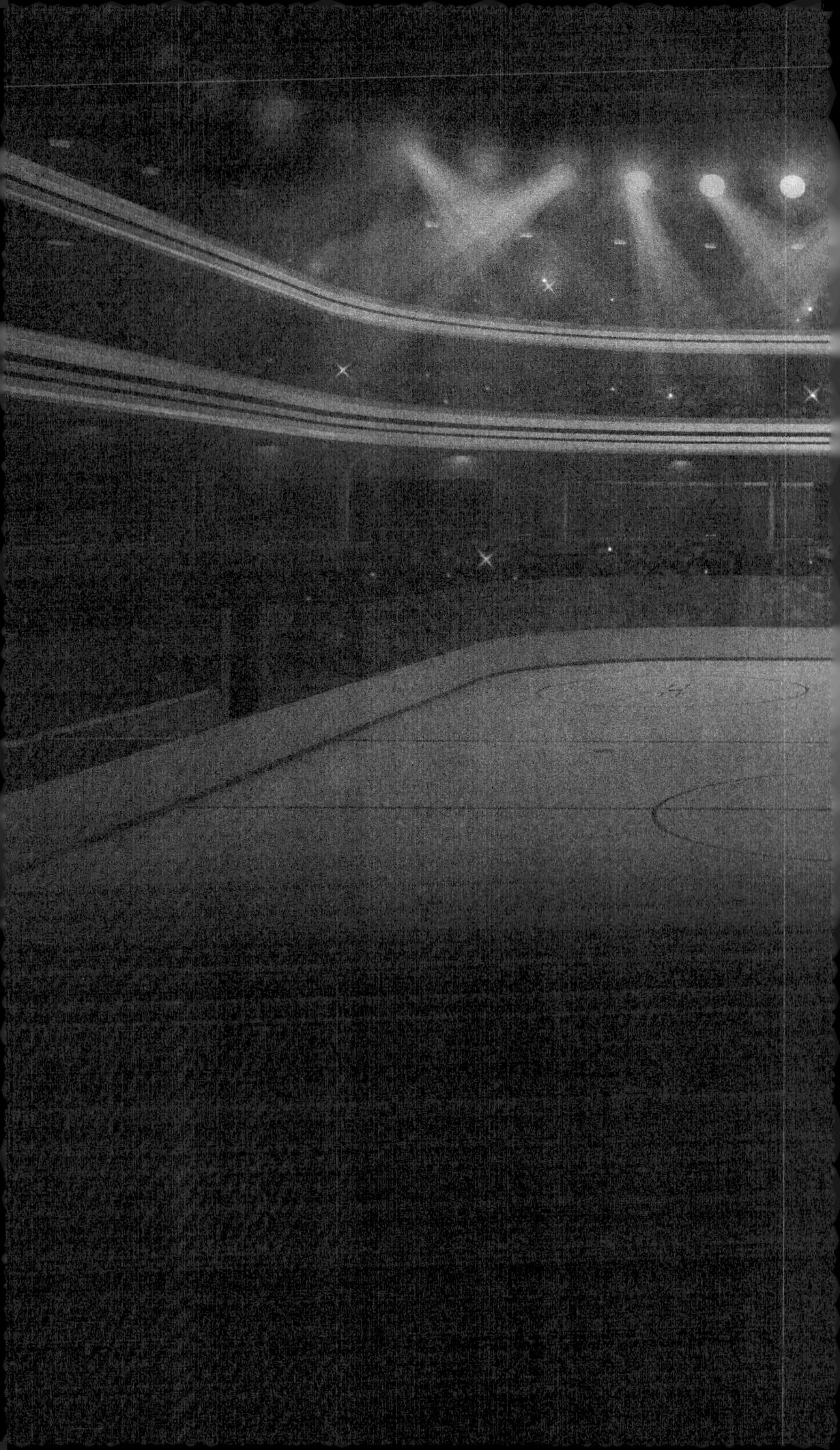

CHAPTER 1

CONNOR

"Fuck yes, this place looks amazing." Noah grinned as he surveyed the house.

It did look pretty dope. The team had turned the place into a living, breathing scare house, and I couldn't wait to see everyone's reactions to our annual Bite the Ice festivities.

It was a team tradition. Every Halloween, the Lakeshore U hockey team transformed Lakers House into the biggest, baddest scare house in town.

"Check this out." I slung my arm around his shoulder and steered him toward the downstairs bathroom door. He frowned at me, and I smirked, "Open it."

Noah rolled his eyes, grabbing the handle and yanking. Wispy tendrils of smoke poured out of the door, a witch's cackle filling the hall as green and white lights flashed from deep within the black void.

"Now that is fucking creepy."

"You're telling me. Took Austin and Linc all day to rig that up. You got a costume?" I asked him.

"Relax, I picked something up."

"Good because if Kellan sees you slacking, he'll make you do lightning drills until your legs fall off."

"He needs to lighten the fuck up."

Kellan was our captain, and he took his job very seriously. Even more so since it was his final year with the team.

And no one loved to give him shit more than our hotheaded rookie, Noah Holden.

"Incoming," someone yelled, and we turned to find Austin and Linc limping a wooden barrel through the house.

"What the fuck?" Noah asked.

"For apple bobbing."

"*Naked* apple bobbing," Austin corrected with a smirk.

"Sounds like my kind of bobbing for apples." Noah held out his fist for Austin, and the two of them laughed. "I sense a lot of pussy in our future. Girls love this shit. The fear and adrenaline—"

"And alcohol. Lots and lots of alcohol." Austin grinned. "It's going to be good times. Good fucking times."

"Hey, maybe Con will end his dry spell," Noah said, and they all looked at me expectantly.

"Fuck off. I told you, it's a new thing I'm trying."

"Has it shriveled up and fallen off yet?"

"No, but your dick will if you keep going bareback, Holden."

"Rule number one, bro," Linc added. "Wrap it before you tap it."

"Fuck off. It was once, and I didn't know she had chlamydia."

Laughter rumbled in my chest. Noah Holden was a force to be reckoned with.

"I'm going to see if the guys need any help upstairs," I said. "Try not to wreck the place before the party gets started."

"Sure thing, *Dad*," Noah called after me as I headed down the hall.

The guys liked to give me shit for being the responsible one—at least, more fucking responsible than most of them—but I didn't mind. I'd done my fair share of partying during freshman year and the first half of sophomore year. But there was more to life than getting wasted and fucking anything in a skirt.

I followed the voices down to the end of the hall and poked my head around the door.

"Ah, Morgan, just the guy we need. Get in here," Kellan said.

"What's up, Cap?"

"This dipshit"—he motioned to Mason—"thought it would be a good idea to rig up a strobe light in here, but he blew the fuse."

"Here, let me take a look." I went over to them and took the plug from Kellan. "I should be able to fix this."

"Knew we could count on you, Morgan," he said. "How are the guys getting on downstairs?"

"It's all coming together."

"You got yourself a costume? I don't want any slackers this year."

"Don't worry, Cap. I understood the assignment." I winked, and he flipped me off.

"Who knows, Morgan," Mase said with a smirk. "Maybe tonight will be your lucky night, and you'll end your dry spell."

"There's nothing wrong with abstaining," Kellan said with a fatherly nod. "Especially so early in the season."

"I beg to differ, Cap. If I go more than a few days without sex, it throws my whole game out of whack."

"You have game?"

"Ouch," Kellan snorted, and Mase flipped us both off.

"And on that note, I'm outta here. I'll see you two assholes tonight."

We watched him disappear into the hall. "We'll need to keep our eyes on Noah and him this season." Kellan let out a heavy sigh. "The last thing we need is two out-of-control rookies."

"Mason is good people."

"He is, but he's easily influenced, and Holden is—"

"A bad influence."

"Potentially." Kellan ran a hand over his jaw. "I don't want anything to screw this season up."

"It won't."

So, some of the guys liked to play hard and party harder. Coach Tucker ran a tight program. So long as it didn't interfere with your performance on the ice or cast a negative light on the team, he was most happy to stay out of our personal lives.

"You're a good, solid guy, Con. I'm glad I get to do this year with you by my side."

"Shit, Cap, don't go getting all emotional on me. We haven't won anything yet."

"No, but I have a good feeling about this season."

"A-fucking-men." We bumped fists.

"Can I leave you to sort this out while I go check on the others? Noah is probably already drinking tonight's stash."

"Sure thing. Leave it with me."

Kellan gave me a small nod before making for the door. But he paused at the last second and glanced back. "You know, she's out there," he said cryptically.

"I have no idea what you're talking about," I said with a coy smile.

"Sure, you don't." Silent laughter danced in his eyes as he slipped into the hall.

Truth was, I'd already met her.

The girl.

The one who I wanted more with.

There was just one huge fucking problem—she wanted nothing to do with me.

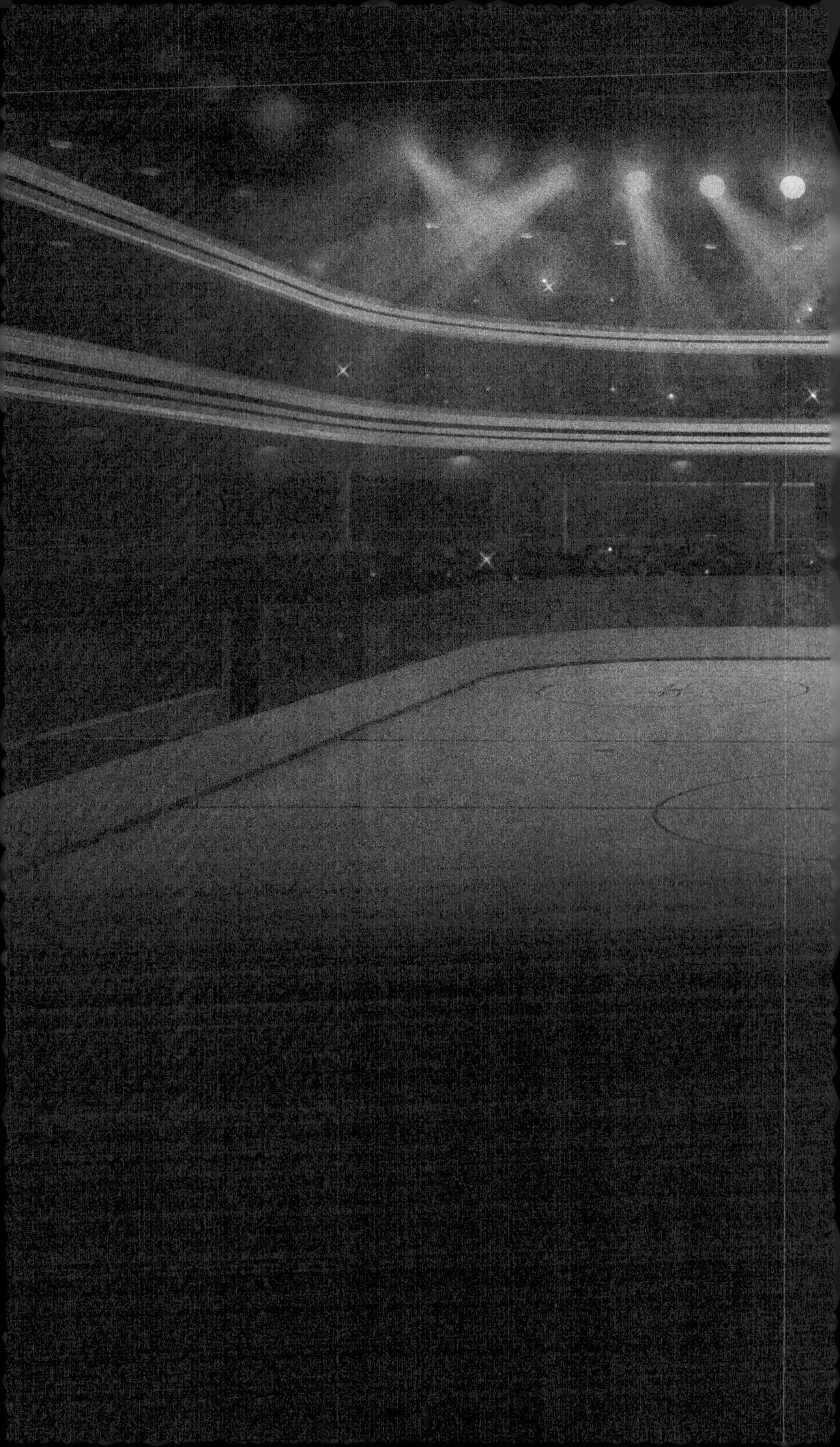

CHAPTER 2

ELLA

"No, absolutely not." I held up my hands, trying to avoid my roommate's attempt at Halloween-ing me. "I hate Halloween."

"I know, I know. And if it weren't for Jolie getting sick, I wouldn't ask. But there's this party, and I really want to go," Maya pouted, flashing me her best puppy-dog impression.

"Where is this party?"

"Uh... Greek row," she rushed out.

"No. No way." I leapt up and headed for the bathroom we shared. "Absolutely not."

"Come on, El. You have to come. Everyone's going

to be there, and I really want to see Noah. We talked again yesterday. He said he liked my boots."

"He was probably imagining you in nothing but said boots," I called over my shoulder. "Noah Holden is one of the biggest players on campus."

"And the hottest."

"I beg to differ," I murmured under my breath.

Noah was hot in that cocky, arrogant, and knows it kind of way. But he flaunted it too much. Smiling and smirking at any girl who crossed his path. The guy only had to blink, and girls fell to their knees, offering to worship him at the altar of his impressive dick if the rumors were to be believed.

I preferred my guys a little less obvious. Not that any of the Lakers hockey players were.

Hockey at Lakeshore U was religion. And everyone worshiped their holy gods.

Not me, though.

I had no intention of ever becoming a puck bunny. Not since freshman year, when I made the fatal error of sleeping with Connor Morgan.

After a handful of dates, I'd thought we had a deep, meaningful connection. But apparently, he thought we'd reached our expiration date and wanted to go out with a bang.

Literally.

God, I could still remember how mortifying it felt to wake up in his bed only to discover he'd left me a note. A fucking *note* saying that he'd had fun and that I could stick around and help myself to breakfast. Like I wanted to stick around and make nice with his housemates after being completely humiliated.

I promised myself that day that I would never get tangled up with a hockey player again. And two years later, here I was. Sticking true to my word.

The Lakeshore U Lakers were a pretty bunch, easy on the eyes and great on the ice, but beyond that, I had no desire to get up close and personal with any of them. Least of all, at some costume party at the team's house on Greek row.

Connor didn't live there; most of the junior and senior players didn't. But it was still Lakers HQ and the regular spot for their parties and general debauchery.

Maya stuck her head around the door, meeting my eyes in the mirror. "Don't you think it's time you let the whole Connor thing go?"

"This has nothing to do with Connor."

"Sure, it doesn't." She rolled her eyes. "You've both dated other people since. You've had at least two relationships, El."

"And that's supposed to somehow negate the fact that he led me on for an entire month only to have sex with me and then dump me? With a note, I might add."

"Yeah, okay, you have a point. The note was a dick move. But he was a freshman. They do dumb shit. He's not that guy anymore. I've heard he doesn't mess around as much now."

"Good for him," bitterness coated my voice.

"El, come on. You were both young. It was freshman year."

She didn't know the truth. How could she when I'd never told a soul before? But I gave myself to Connor that night.

I was a virgin, and I trusted him with my body—and heart.

And he crushed me.

"I don't care about Connor," I said, feeling the lie snake through me.

"So then, there's no reason not to come to the party. It's junior year, babe. We need to party while we still can before classes get too intense. You know the team rigged up the house with all these booby traps and scary decorations. It'll be fun."

"Maya…"

"El." Her pout grew. "Aren't you at least a little bit curious about Connor and what he's like now?"

I knew enough about Connor Morgan to last me a lifetime, but she wasn't going to let it drop.

Maya was stubborn to boot. And maybe she had a point. Two years had passed. I didn't have to avoid the hockey team forever. He probably didn't even remember me.

My stomach dipped.

How depressing.

Connor probably didn't even remember me, and I'd spent the last two years comparing every guy I dated to my first and only time with him.

"Fine," I said. "I'll come. But I need a costume."

"Did you think I'd brought the cat ears for fun?" Maya grinned, tugging me back into the living room. "This is going to be so much fun."

"Fun, yeah," I murmured. "I'll believe it when I see it."

"So negative." She stuck out her tongue at me. "I have a good feeling about tonight, El. Maybe you'll finally meet your prince."

I highly doubted that was possible at a frat house full of drunken, immoral hockey players.

But I didn't argue.

Instead, I accepted the costume from Maya and begrudgingly changed into it. If I was going to grace the Lakers House with my presence, I was going to look damn hot doing it.

We didn't even make it to the door before we were intercepted by a zombie hockey player. He slung his arm around Maya, and she giggled up at him.

"Meow, who's your friend?" His eyes were trained on me, not her.

"Oh, this is El."

"Nice outfit."

"Thanks." My lips thinned as I scanned the scene before me. People all dressed to be someone—or something—else spilled out of the house, music pouring out the door and windows. Skeletons hung from the porch, fake cobwebs strung up in the corners, stretching to the front door. It was effective; I'd give them that. But anyone could grab a few supplies from Target and turn their house into a place of nightmares.

"Unimpressed?" he asked me.

"It looks great." I shot him a saccharine smile.

"Is Noah inside?" Maya asked.

"Uh, Holden is around." The guy's eyes flared with something.

"Around? What does that mean?"

"It means he's around." He grinned, letting his glassy eyes fall down my body. It had been a while since I'd had the attention of a guy, but it did little for me.

He was a hockey player, and I was... so not interested. Besides, these guys fucked anything in a skirt. It wasn't exactly a confidence booster to pass their questionable standards.

"I need a drink," I said, making for the door.

"See you around." Maya joined me, giving me a smile. "Ready?"

"As I'll ever be."

She rang the skull and crossbones door knocker, and the door swung open, revealing the grim reaper. "Welcome to Bite the Ice." He handed us a glass of bright green liquid.

"I'm not drinking that," I said.

"Suit yourself." He shrugged, snatching my glass back. "Shall we?" His gaze fixed on Maya.

"On three," she grinned.

"Ma—"

"One. Two. Three." They both downed the mysterious drink, and Maya chuckled.

"It's just punch, El."

"El?" The guy narrowed his eyes at me. "Ella

Henshaw?"

"Yeah, what of it?"

"Connor's El?"

"Excuse me?" My stomach plummeted into my toes.

"I... uh, nothing. Nothing. Forget I said anything."

My gaze slid to Maya in question, and she shrugged. "Come on. I want to find Noah."

The grim reaper let us past, and we slipped into the smoky shadows.

"Wow, they really went all out," I said over the music as I surveyed the house.

The place was crowded, girls and guys pressed in close, drinking, dancing, making out in dark corners.

A flash of heat went through me. It had been a while since I'd been to a party like this. I tended to avoid the college party scene, preferring drinks with the girls and dancing at one of the downtown bars.

Maya grabbed my hand and tugged me further down the hall into the huge open-plan kitchen. A loud cheer went up in the air, and I instantly found the source of the commotion.

A beer pong table had been set up on the opposite side of the room, in front of the open patio doors that led to the impressive yard.

The guys weren't throwing regular balls, though;

they were playing with eyeballs, complete with dangling optic nerves.

"That is... ew," Maya chuckled. "Shall we get a drink?"

"Something in a bottle," I said, and she frowned. "Come on, El. The guys don't let anyone do that shit."

I shrugged. "You can't be too careful." And the last thing I wanted was to end up roofied at a frat party I didn't want to be at in the first place.

"You need to learn to live a little, girl," Maya smirked. "You also need to get back on the horse."

"Maya," I hissed, glancing around to make sure no one could hear her.

"You haven't had sex since Rich if you can call it sex."

"He wasn't that bad."

"Really?" She deadpanned. "The guy was so vanilla he wouldn't know what to do with the whole ice cream sundae."

"So he liked missionary." With the light off, after a shower.

Ugh.

She was right, and I hated it. Hated that I'd wasted four months of my life on a guy who was such a disappointment in the bedroom that my vagina had officially closed up shop when we broke up.

"Babe, you deserve good sex. Hot, sweaty, downright dirty sex. Your vagina deserves some love. She deserves— Connor."

"What? No, absolutely not. Have you lost your goddamn mi—" Maya fought a smile, her eyes widening over my shoulder, and realization slammed into me. "He's behind me, isn't he?" I murmured, wishing the floor would open up and swallow me whole.

A trickle of awareness spread through me as I turned slowly to meet Connor's steely gaze.

"Ella Henshaw, this is a surprise." A slight smirk played on his lips.

"Connor Morgan."

"Long time no see."

"Not long enough," I mumbled, and Maya gave me a disapproving nudge.

"I can see I've got my work cut out for me." He rubbed his jaw, making no effort to disguise the way his intense gaze swept down my body, igniting a firestorm inside me.

Connor always did have a strange effect on me.

It's why I'd fallen for him in the first place—why I'd gone against everything I knew about hockey players and given him a chance.

I wasn't the same naïve freshman I was back then, though.

"You look good, El." His eyes twinkled, but I shored up my defenses.

"So do you. Good to see you, Connor. We were just leaving." I grabbed Maya and practically dragged her from the kitchen.

Connor's deep laughter chasing me the hell out of there.

CHAPTER 3

CONNOR

"Jesus, your girl looks fine." Austin clapped me on the back as we watched Ella drag her friend from the kitchen.

I let out a heavy sigh, "She's not my girl."

"Yet. She's not your girl yet." He grinned. "Think positive, Con. This could be your shot."

I wasn't so sure about that.

Ella Henshaw hated me with a fiery passion that I felt every single time we crossed paths around campus. And it wasn't all that much, considering she went out of her way to avoid me.

But she was my biggest regret.

The one that got away.

And by the time I realized it, I'd lost her.

That was two years ago, and I'd had a string of meaningless hookups and bad dates since. But not a single one of them had erased the memory of Ella.

I'd fucked up the night I'd finally got her underneath me, but I'd panicked. I was a freshman, a rookie looking to make his mark on the team. I didn't have time for a girlfriend. It was the one thing Coach Tucker consistently drilled into us—no distractions. And Ella Henshaw was the worst kind.

So I ended it before we got in too deep. Looking back, I could see what a dick move it was to sleep with her and leave her with just a note.

A fucking note.

I was an idiot.

But I had more important things to think about back then.

"Come on," I said, forcing myself to stop staring at the door where Ella and her friend had long disappeared through. "Let's get a drink."

Slinging my arm around Austin's shoulder, I guided him back toward the huge island. Bottles of liquor were scattered in and amongst buckets of dry ice and spooky green and black lights. The effect was freaky as fuck, but it didn't stop me from plucking two bottles of Heineken from a bucket.

"Here." I handed him one.

"Con, Austin, you guys in the next round?" Mase called from the beer pong table.

"Count me in," Austin said.

"Con?"

"Nah, I'm good." My focus was shot after seeing Ella in that sexy as fuck kitten outfit.

"Lover boy's girl showed up," Austin said, and I groaned into my hand.

"That Ella chick?" Linc grinned. "She came?"

"Pretty sure she'd rather not be here," I murmured.

I hadn't seen her at a Lakers party—or any party around campus for that matter—in the two years since we'd hooked up.

"But she is, so the question now is, what the fuck are you going to do about it?"

The guys all stared at me expectantly. After I stupidly got drunk and confessed my one-that-got-away story over the summer, they'd all given me shit about it. Noah, the little shit, wanted to go directly to the source and woo her on my behalf.

Fucking idiot.

I'd warned them all off. If—and it was a big if—Ella ever gave me another chance, I wasn't looking to play games.

Two years.

I'd waited two fucking years for this moment. I sure as shit wasn't about to let the guys screw it up for me.

"Hey, what did I miss?" Aiden Dumfries appeared out of nowhere in that usual way of his.

The team was tight. Bonded over their love of hockey and puck bunnies mostly. But Aiden was an enigma. Angry and bitter, he used all his bad energy out on the ice to crush our opponents. And nine times out of ten, it worked.

"Morgan's crush is here," Austin said through a shit-eating grin. "He's finally decided to hand his balls to a member of the fairer sex."

"Seriously? You like a girl?" Aiden gawked at me.

"So what if I do?" I bristled.

"Huh. Nothing. Just didn't see that one coming." He clapped me on the back. "Well, good luck, I guess. Although, it sounds like your funeral, if you ask me."

"Nobody did ask you, Dumfries." Asshole.

I liked the guy, and he was an incredible player. But there was something about it that made him hard to get to know. Probably had something to do with the fact his old man was a con artist who had made local news more than once. Aiden acted indifferent to it all, but that shit had to stick.

"Gotta agree with Dumfries, Con," Noah piped up. "Too many puck bunnies on the ice to settle down."

The little shit would say that. He went through women faster than Dumfries went through new sticks.

I drained my beer and made my excuses. Ella was here somewhere, and I wanted to talk to her.

Before she disappeared from my life again for the next two years.

I moved from room to room, trying to spot a flash of cat ears. But the place was crowded, huddles of overexcited girls shrieking at every turn, thanks to the booby traps and decorations.

Even I got into a fight with a full-sized skeleton when I went into the game room.

"Connor, there you are," a voice called after me, and I turned to find Melissa Dukes flashing me more than just a smile.

"I've been looking for you," she said, batting her fake eyelashes at me.

"Hey, Mel. How are you enjoying the party?"

She stepped closer, running a manicured nail up

my chest. "I think my night will be a whole lot better now you're here."

"Actually," I gently pried her hand off my shirt. "I'm looking for somebody."

"Oh." Dejection flashed in her eyes.

Melissa and I had hooked up a handful of times last year. She was less intense than some of the puck bunnies that hung around, happy to keep things casual and make no promises. But from the possessive glint in her eyes, I was wondering if I'd misread the situation.

"Enjoy the party," I said, moving around her. Because if I'd learned anything since arriving at LU, it was when to walk away from a pretty girl with stars in her eyes.

I continued my search, working through the last two rooms on the first floor. The living room and the gym.

The second I stepped into the gym, or the graveyard as it had been transformed into for tonight, I found her. All the equipment had been moved to the edge of the room and covered in black sheets to create the graveyard perimeter. Plastic fake headstones were planted throughout the space and a smoke machine pumped out a constant trickle of fog along the floor.

But I didn't care about any of that. I only had eyes

for the woman dancing in that ridiculously sexy costume of hers. The skintight black pants and halter top might as well have been painted on for how little it left to the imagination. Every curve was on full display as Ella danced with her friend. I leaned against a treadmill, watching her. Transfixed on the way her hips swayed and moved to the sultry beat.

Ella Henshaw was the hottest girl I'd ever laid eyes on, and I was a fool for ever letting her walk away. But I was a different guy back then. Young and foolish. Consumed with the idea of hockey stardom. Coach liked to remind us of the danger of distractions, but what he didn't realize was that half the guys on the team were distracted by the endless offers of casual sex and parties and college debauchery. So long as it didn't affect their performance on the ice, he didn't care.

But the last few months, I'd been wondering if we were missing a trick. Having a girlfriend wasn't a distraction. Not if she was the *right* girl.

And I couldn't get Ella out of my head. I saw her around campus, watched her in the coffee shop sometimes, and even found excuses to go by the library just to catch a glimpse of her working a shift. But I never approached her.

Until tonight.

Because as my mom had insisted on drilling into me, you shouldn't play with a girl's heart unless you had plans to keep it.

I wanted Ella Henshaw.

And tonight, was the night I was finally going to make her mine.

At least, that was the plan.

Ella's friend spotted me first, her lip curving into a surprised grin as she shot me an encouraging wink. Leaning in, she whispered something to Ella, who instantly frowned. The two of them seemed to argue, and then her friend took off, disappearing out of the room.

Before Ella could go after her, I slipped up behind her, wrapping an arm around her waist. Her whole body froze up, and I whispered, "It's me."

"Connor?" A shudder ran through her.

"Dance with me, kitten?"

"In case you have forgotten, I hate you."

"Dance with me, please."

She let out a breathy sigh. "One dance."

Bingo.

Smiling to myself, I walked backward a little, pulling Ella into a shadowy corner of the room. Tucking her against my chest, I started moving us to the beat.

Ella was tense at first, moving stiffly. But slowly, as the song went on, she began to relax until her perfect body rolled and popped against mine.

Jesus, she felt good: all soft curves and even softer skin. I let my hand trace her arm, reveling in how a shiver rolled through her entire body.

"Connor," she whispered.

"Shh, baby. I got you." Brushing the hair off her shoulder, I ghosted my lips over the crook of her neck, barely touching her.

It wasn't enough. Nowhere near enough. But I didn't want to scare her away, not when I finally had her in my arms.

Mom always said I'd know it when I found the woman for me. I'd known it that night two years ago, just like I knew it now.

Ella Henshaw was mine.

I'd just been too fucking chickenshit to do anything about it back then.

My dick strained painfully behind my pants' zipper as if it knew too. That she was ours. That she belonged to us.

The corner of my mouth tipped up as I nuzzled her neck, swaying us to the beat.

"I've been waiting a long time for this," I said, turning her in my arms. Touching my head to hers, I breathed her in.

"You don't mean that." She stared at me with something like awe and confusion.

"I'm serious." My hand slid into the back of her hair and held her nape.

"You're drunk."

"I'm sober as a judge."

"It won't work, you know. I fell for the Connor Morgan charm once before. I won't fall for it again." Her brows knitted together in an adorable frown. But she was still here, making no move to escape.

That had to mean something, didn't it?

But then I went and said the one thing that could screw up my chance before she even agreed to give me one.

"I never forgot that night, kitten," I confessed. "Not for a second."

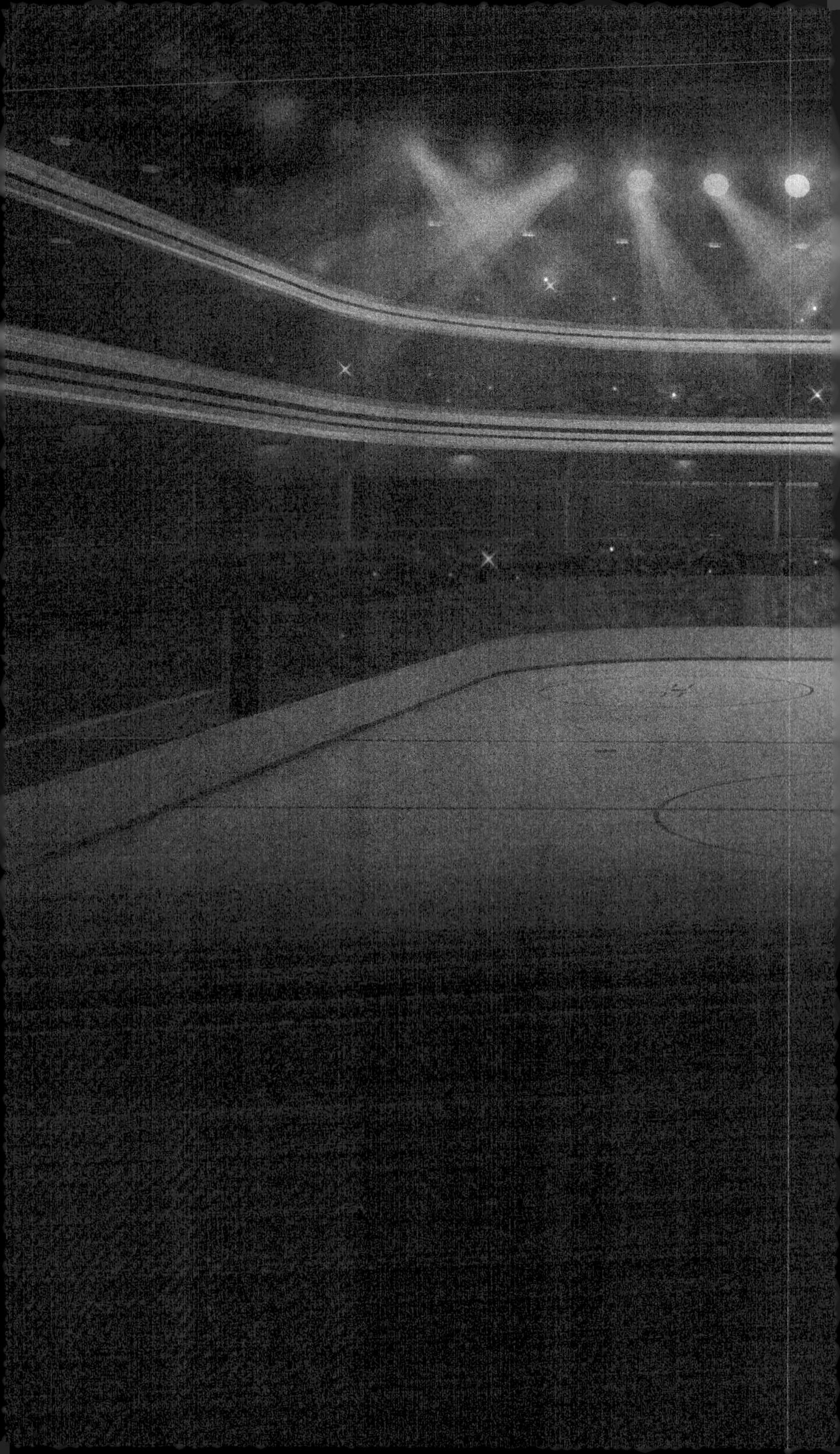

CHAPTER 4

ELLA

My heart crashed violently in my chest as Connor held me, running his hands up and down my waist almost reverently.

I wasn't supposed to be here, at this party—a hockey party of all things—dancing with Connor.

But he made it hard to resist. That and the alcohol coursing through my bloodstream.

I've been waiting a long time for this. His confession played over in my mind. Surely, it was a line. Some cheap trick to get me to lower my defenses. Because it was Connor freaking Morgan, he could have any girl on campus he wanted—probably already had.

Ugh. I shut that thought down as quickly as it had entered my head.

"You don't believe me," he said, the spark shuttering in his eyes a little.

"It was two years ago."

"What can I say? You left a mark."

"I left a... let me go." I tried to shirk out of his hold, but Connor grabbed my arms. Not forcefully but tight enough that I couldn't escape.

"I fucked up that night, kitten. Got a real bad case of cold feet."

Cold feet, was he for real?

"So what? You thought you'd wait two years to confess all this to me in hopes of what, winning me over?"

"Is it working?" He flashed me a crooked grin, and I found myself laughing because he was being so ridiculous.

We were at a party, a Lakers party, in a house full of drunk hockey players and the girls and guys who worshiped the ice they played on, and Connor seriously expected me to believe that he wanted me.

After all this time.

"Okay, how much?"

"Huh?" His brows knitted.

"How much is the bet?"

"Bet, you think... shit, El. This isn't about no bet. I'm serious."

"But it doesn't make any sense. You slept with me and then ghosted me."

"I left a note."

"Exactly. You took my... We had sex, and you left a note."

His eyes narrowed. "What did you just say."

"We had sex—"

"Before that?"

"Nothing. I didn't say anything." Panic clawed up inside me. "Thanks for the dance, but I really have to go."

This time when I tried to wriggle out of his hold, Connor let me go. I didn't look back as I weaved through the bodies and fled the room.

God, I hadn't meant to let that slip out. He didn't need to know what that night meant to me. But I couldn't catch a break. No sooner had I reached the end of the hall had Connor caught up to me and pulled me into the bathroom.

A witch's cackle filled the room, ringing in my ears as the lights flashed around us.

"Ella, baby, please tell me you weren't about to say what I think you were going to say." Pain flashed in his eyes.

"I..." Nope. He didn't deserve the truth.

He didn't deserve me.

I pressed my lips together as he crowded me against the wall. It was dark, eerie, with a thick layer of smoke rising around us. I knew it was nothing more than some trick lighting and a smoke machine, but it didn't stop my heart from going wild.

"Kitten, talk to me." He cupped my face, fixing my eyes on his as he brushed my cheek with his thumb. "Tell me the truth."

"Why? It doesn't change anything."

"If you were about to say what I think you were, it changes everything. Every-fucking-thing."

"Fine," I snapped. "I gave myself to you, and you cast me aside like I was nothing more than a cheap lay. There, does that make you feel better? Does that—"

His hand glided down the side of my neck to wrap around my throat.

"Con, what are—"

"Gonna kiss you now," he murmured, his mouth crashing down on mine, stealing my breath. Heat pooled in my stomach, desire pulsing through me.

I hadn't felt this in so long.

And somewhere in the back of my lust-addled mind, I knew it was all his fault. After he'd ghosted me, I rallied my defenses, buried my heart under a thick layer of ice. I became guarded and wary. I couldn't trust anyone. And that always got in the way when it came to being intimate.

But this was Connor. I already knew that he'd break my heart. Yet, my body, my non-existent sex life, clearly hadn't gotten the memo.

"Fuck, you're sexy." His hand snaked around my body and grabbed my ass. "I can't get enough of you in this outfit."

"Connor," I breathed. "What are we doing?"

He ghosted his lips over mine, smiling. "Making up for lost time."

"In the Lakers House bathroom?"

"We can get out of here? Go somewhere a little more private?" His eyes burned with hunger, all of it aimed right at me.

I didn't want to do this, did I?

But he felt so good; his big, strong body pressed up against mine. The way he handled me with total confidence. The smidge of cocky arrogance oozed from him.

I was falling hook, line, and sinker for Connor Morgan's charm.

And maybe it was the liquor in my veins, or maybe it was the Halloween magic in the air, but I couldn't find it in myself to care.

"Where are we going?" I asked, pressing myself into Connor's side as he guided me down the hall toward the staircase.

"You'll see."

"Connor, maybe—"

"No." He pressed a finger to my lips. "We are doing this. Me and you. Tonight."

Something about the longing in his voice, the sheer desperation, made my stomach clench.

"Besides," he added. "If you turn me down, I'm going to spend the rest of the night watching your every move to make sure none of the other assholes here try to make a move on my girl."

His girl...

His girl?

What was happening?

"Come on." He grinned, tugging me up the stairs.

Nervous energy bounced around my stomach, but I felt strangely at ease with him.

We reached the end of the hall, and Connor opened the door.

"Please tell me we're not about to borrow one of your teammate's bedrooms. Because that—"

"Kitten?" He pressed his face right up against mine.

My breath caught at his sudden proximity. "Y-yeah?"

"Stop overthinking it."

Connor pulled me inside, closing the door, and the air shifted around us. Thick with anticipation.

"You were a virgin."

I nodded, my cheeks burning with the confession.

"Fuck, El. I'm so fucking sorry. I didn't know. I didn't—"

"I was a virgin, Connor, not a saint."

A low growl rumbled in his chest, and I giggled, "Did you just... growl?"

"Don't like the idea of you with anyone else, kitten."

"So you haven't dated or been with anyone else since me?"

"Shit, baby. You know I have. A lot of faceless girls, I can't remember. But that's not who I am anymore. It's not what I want..."

"What do you want, Connor?"

"Honestly? Without coming off any more creeper-like than I already have? You, Ella. I want a second shot with you."

"But... Why?"

He had his shot two years ago, and he blew it. He didn't only blow it; he broke my naïve freshman heart, who thought mind-blowing sex would lead to a long and happy relationship.

"Because I was a fool." He smiled, and it did things to my heart. Stupid, reckless things. "A hopeless idiot who let his girl slip through his fingers." He buried his hand in my hair, stroking along my skin.

My eyelids fluttered as a shudder went through me. Jesus, he was saying and doing all the right things.

But I couldn't believe him, could I?

"You're... a Laker. You guys don't do relationships."

"Maybe I want to start a new trend." He smiled, and I found myself smiling back.

"You're making it really hard for me to say no, Connor."

"So say yes, El. Give me another chance."

"One night," I breathed, hardly able to believe I'd said the words. "You get one night. But I swear to God, Connor, if you leave me another note..."

I wouldn't survive it again.

"How does breakfast sound instead?"

"Hmm." I brushed my lips over the corner of his mouth. "Who said anything about sleeping over?"

"You said one night, kitten, and I want the whole damn night."

Oh my.

I was in trouble.

So much freaking trouble.

"Fine. You get the whole night," I smirked. "Make it count."

CHAPTER 5

CONNOR

ELLA GAZED UP AT ME, a heady mix of lust and surprise shining in her eyes.

Yes.

She'd said yes.

I had been prepared to beg, to get on my knees and convince her to give me another shot. But she'd said yes.

One night. She was giving me one whole night. I didn't tell her that I wanted more than that—I didn't want to scare her away. If things went how I hoped they would, though, and I got my way, tonight would be the start of something more.

Shit, what if she saw this as closure? As a way to finally cut me out of her life forever?

Fuck that.

I'd waited two years to make my move. I wasn't about to let her sabotage my plans. I just had to make every second count. I had to show her how fucking good we could be together.

I had to turn on the Connor Morgan charm.

"Say something," she whispered, running her hand over my shoulder and along the back of my neck. Such an intimate action. Familiar and comforting. I wondered if she knew that.

Knew how fucking right it felt.

"You are so fucking beautiful," I said, brushing my thumb down her cheek and over her lips, letting it drag slowly across the pillow of her bottom lip.

Ella sucked in a sharp breath, a shiver going through her.

"Are you going to stand there all night looking at me? Or are you going to kiss me?"

Fuck. I didn't need to be asked twice.

Burying my hand in her hair, I angled Ella's face to mine and kissed her. Slow and deep, tangling our tongues together. She responded, becoming soft and pliant in my hands.

"Connor," she breathed, breaking away to try and

catch her breath. But I couldn't stop; I couldn't get enough.

I smashed my mouth down on hers, plunging my tongue into her mouth as I grabbed the backs of her thighs and hauled her against me. Ella's thighs fell open, letting me wrap her legs around my waist and carry her to the nearest wall. Her hands went into my hair, nails scraping along my scalp, making my heart beat out of my fucking chest.

I pressed her into the wall, trapping her with my body. My dick was rock hard, desperate to be reacquainted with the only girl I'd ever thought about after being with her.

Two years of fantasizing about Ella, wondering how different things might have been if I'd only been brave enough to stick around. She was here now, though, and I had no intention of squandering my shot at showing her how I felt.

I ground into her, groaning at the heat of her pussy as she rubbed herself on me.

"Connor, touch me. I need for you to touch me."

That was going to be a problem, given the skintight pants she had on. So I swung her around and carried her to the bed, laying her down. Ella twisted her fingers into my black t-shirt and pulled me down on top of her, kissing the shit out of me.

Damn, I liked this side of her. Confident and unafraid to take what she wanted. I only hoped that when the sun came up and the dust settled, that she still wanted me.

Breaking the kiss, I gazed down at her, and she frowned. "What?"

"I can't believe you're here."

"Shut up and kiss me." She went to yank me to her again, but I resisted.

"I believe you asked me to touch you." I slid a hand between our bodies and cupped her pussy, running a finger along the seam of her pants.

She gasped, her eyes wide and burning with desire.

"Let's get you out of those ridiculously sexy pants. Kitten," I crooned, moving down her body and dropping to the foot of the bed.

Ella propped herself up on her elbows, watching me intently as I took off her sexy heels and slowly peeled off her pants, and threw them to the side.

Fuck. She was stunning—all soft curves and smooth skin. I ran a hand up her leg, ankle to thigh. She fell back onto the mattress, my name a breathy sigh on her lips.

I smoothed my hands over her stomach and down to her thighs, spreading her open for me.

Her black lacy panties taunted me, begging me to have a taste, so I lowered my mouth to her pussy, blowing a stream of hot air along the seam.

"Oh, Con." She arched into me, seeking more. Her fingers slid into my hair as I pressed open-mouthed kisses all over her. I wanted her hot and desperate, delirious with need. I wanted to feast on her until she was begging, fucking begging me to take her.

"More," she panted, trying to guide my head to where she wanted me. But I held back, teasing her, licking and nibbling her through the sexy as fuck lace.

"Conner, stop teasing me, and touch me."

"Yes, ma'am," I chuckled, dragging her panties off her body and shoving them in my pocket.

I stood, making quick work of stripping out of my vampire costume. But I left my boxers on. If she wanted me bare, she could be the one to strip me naked.

Ella's eyes danced over my body, lingering on my chest. "So unfair," she murmured, and I smirked, smoothing a hand over my stomach.

"I work hard to look this good."

"Yeah, yeah, Morgan, tell it to somebody who cares."

"I think you'll care when I'm fucking you senseless."

"Connor, you can't—"

I dropped to my knees, throwing her legs over my shoulder, and buried my face in her pussy, licking her.

"Jesus H. Christ," she moaned, writhing against me.

I used my fingers to spread her open, so I could dip my tongue into her, spreading her arousal around before flattening my tongue against her clit.

She tasted like fucking heaven, and something settled deep inside me.

This woman was mine.

I'd let her slip through my fingers once, but it wasn't going to happen again.

I ate her until she was moaning my name, praising me like a god. Fumbling on the floor beside me, I managed to reach for my wallet and grab a condom while bringing her closer to the edge.

"Yes, oh God... yes..." Ella's fingers tightened into my hair to the point of pain. But I didn't care. Watching her come undone for me was one of the sexiest things I'd ever witnessed.

"Give it to me, kitten. I want to feel you come all over my tongue." I dipped it inside her again, rubbing her clit in hard little circles. Her body began to quiver, her thighs locking around my head as she came with a whimper.

Crawling up her body, I kissed her, letting her taste herself on my tongue.

"That was amazing," she whispered, her eyes heavy-lidded.

"You haven't seen anything yet." Anchoring her to my body, I flipped us over, settling her on top of me.

"Connor..."

"I want to watch as I fuck you, kitten. I'm yours; whatever you need, take it."

A needy whimper slipped from her lips as I thrust up a little and grabbed her ass, pulling her right over my dick, letting her feel how turned on I was.

"Your body is a work of art." Ella ran her hands all over me, dragging her fingers along the hard ridges of my stomach.

"My best feature is about four inches lower," I drawled. Although I would die a happy man like this, having her hands on my skin and her smile aimed in my direction.

I couldn't even imagine how good it would feel to be inside her again.

Ella got off me and made easy work of ridding me of my boxers. When she settled back over my thighs, she surprised the fuck out of me by fisting my dick.

"Hmm," she purred. "Just as perfect as I remember."

"You been dreaming of my dick, baby?"

"Don't ruin it, Connor." Her lips pursed, but I saw the glint of mischief in her eyes. She pumped me root to tip. Once. Twice. Adding a little twist on the upstroke that made me groan.

"Feels so fucking good."

"What about this?" She rose on her knees and leaned forward, sliding the tip through her wetness.

"Jesus, El," I choked out. Her warm, wet heat almost short-circuiting my brain.

She did it again, rocking a little, adding more pressure. If I didn't get inside her in the next ten seconds, there was every chance this would be over before it even got started.

"Put me inside you, kitten. I need to feel you."

Ella didn't fight me on it, and there was something so fucking sexy about the way she tore open the foil packet with her teeth and expertly rolled the latex over my shaft.

I didn't want to think about how—*or who*—she'd had so much practice with. Not that it mattered when I was one second away from fucking out every guy who had come before tonight right from her mind.

Gripping Ella's hips, I steadied her as she grasped my dick and slowly sank down on me. "Fuuuuck," I hissed, my eyes rolling back with sheer pleasure. She felt so fucking good I had to force air into my lungs.

"Oh God," she whimpered, grinding on me until I was fully seated inside her.

Grabbing her by the nape, I pulled Ella down to kiss her. She clenched, tightening around me, and we both groaned. "Fuck me, baby. Use me."

Anchoring her hand around the back of my neck, Ella touched her head to mine as she began riding me. "Why does it feel so good?" Her voice was cracked with lust.

"Because you were made for me."

I was laying it on thick, saying things I'd never said to another girl. But it felt right. It felt like a defining point in my life.

"Connor," she breathed, rocking her hips faster... harder.

I sat up, pressing us together. It was deeper like this, more intense, but I could touch her body now. Run my hands over her silky skin, take in the perfection of her soft curves.

"It's too much," she cried.

"You can take it," I said, gathering her hair in my fist so I could kiss her shoulder.

"It's so good. It feels... ah..."

I captured her mouth in another bruising kiss,

swallowing her moans of pleasure, the tiny whimpers of desperation as we both raced toward the edge.

"You think you can come for me again, baby?"

Ella nodded, her eyes glazed over as she bounced on my dick, using my body for leverage as she lifted up and slammed back down.

"Need some help?" I slipped a hand between our bodies and found her clit, massaging it.

"Oh God," Ella panted, her body trembling. "I'm so close, Con. I'm so..." Her cries filled the room as she came, her pussy rippling around me.

"That's it, kitten. Give it to me. Give." *Thrust.* "It." *Thrust.* "To." *Thrust.* "Me."

Pleasure barreled down my spine as an orgasm slammed into me. I gathered Ella to me, needing her as close as possible while we rode out the lingering waves of ecstasy.

"Amazing," I said. "You are amazing."

It had never been this good before. Only one time came close, and that was two years ago with this very woman.

"Connor," she murmured, crashing in my arms.

"Come on, let's get you into bed." I swung my legs off the bed and stood with her wrapped around me like a koala.

Pulling back the sheets, I lay Ella down. "I'll be just a minute."

I made quick work of discarding the condom and climbing into bed with her. Ella nestled into my side, and I slipped an arm around her, loving the way she felt pressed against me.

"Give me twenty minutes, and we can go again."

Her soft laughter filled the room. "I might need a little longer to recover," she said quietly.

"You're tired?"

"A little."

"Close your eyes then. I'll be right here when you wake. Because you promised me the night, and I'm not done with you yet." I kissed her hair, and she let out a contented sigh. "

We had the whole night; a breather wouldn't hurt.

But when I woke four hours later and reached for her warm body, I found the bedsheets stone cold...

And Ella was gone.

CHAPTER 6

ELLA

"I can't believe you had sex with Connor Morgan. Ah, El, this is so fucking exciting." Maya clapped her hands together, grinning like a fool.

"Don't start planning the wedding just yet. I got spooked and ran out of there before we could do the awkward morning after thing."

Her expression sobered. "Yeah, what's up with that? I thought you said it was the best sex of your life."

That was half the problem. It had been too good. Too easy. Too freaking right.

When I'd woken wrapped up in Connor's big strong arms, I'd panicked. Everything had been perfect between us. But it was one night, not the first night of something more. I'd made that mistake before; I wasn't about to make it again.

So I'd hurried out of there without waking him.

"It was," I said. "But it was only sex, Maya."

"Bullshit. You like him. I remember how badly you were hurt when he left that note. You thought he was Mr. Right."

"Yeah, well, I was young and naïve." I stared out the window. Campus was finally stirring after a heavy night of parties.

"Oh, El," she sighed. "You didn't even stick around to see where his head was at."

"Because it was just sex."

Sure, Connor had said and done all the right things, but we were caught up in the moment, the natural chemistry we shared getting the better of us.

He was Connor Morgan, for Pete's sake, one of the Lakers star players. He didn't want a serious relationship. It was all talk. All part of his plan to lure me into false pretenses and get me beneath him again.

I didn't mind that part so much. The sex had been life-altering. Cosmic. And I'd needed it. But that was it; it was done.

Over.

We could both move on with our lives.

A hollow feeling went through me. If only he'd been a scholar instead of an athlete, maybe we would have stood a chance. But as it was, I couldn't compete with hockey and everything that came with it.

No. I needed to commit the night to memory and accept it for what it was: the best sex of my life.

"I think you're wrong," Maya said defiantly. "I saw the way he looked at you. It wasn't just sex. He likes you, really likes you."

"Will you stop already?"

"Fine. But something tells me that isn't the last you'll see of Connor Morgan, El."

"Whatever," I murmured, focusing my attention on the textbook in front of me.

Maya got up and went over to our shared kitchen area. "You know, El. It's okay if you do like him."

"Thanks for that, but I don't."

"Okay, if you say so."

"I do."

"Okay."

"Okay." My eyes narrowed at her, and she smiled.

"I'm going to the gym. See you later."

"Don't work too hard," I called as she grabbed her bag and headed for the door.

"I'll try not to."

Her laughter lingered as she slipped out of our

apartment. But it was her words that stuck with me long after she'd gone.

Thanks to Maya and her sage words of advice, I couldn't concentrate. So what if I did like Connor? It wasn't like he actually meant anything he said last night.

It was just sex.

Hot, sweaty, intense sex.

I could still feel the ache between my thighs, and it had been hours since I fled the Lakers House.

Ugh. I had no hopes of concentrating with images of us together infiltrating my mind. It had been so good.

Too good.

Easier than any moments of intimacy I'd have had with another guy. Why, why, why did I have to be so attracted to him?

A knock on the apartment door pulled me from my thoughts, and I got up, frowning. It was probably Maya. She always forgot her key.

"Seriously, again?" I called, going to the door. "You're going to— Connor."

He stood there in a Lakers jersey, smiling down at me.

"W-what are you doing here?"

"You ran," he said, his mouth twitching.

"I... sorry, what?"

"You promised me the whole night, and you ran."

"Connor, come on. You didn't... we didn't..."

"Cat got your tongue, baby?" He took a step forward, and I inched back.

"What are you doing?"

"Coming in."

"No, I don't think that's a good idea." He was here. At my door. Looking every bit as gorgeous as I remembered.

"I am coming in, kitten. You and I need to talk."

"Wha—" But Connor slipped past me and made a beeline for the couch.

"Come in," I murmured, irritation trickling down my spine. "Make yourself at home."

"Nice place," he said with a small grin.

I let out a heavy sigh and went over to the couch. But I remained standing. "Well..."

"Are you always this friendly when you have guests over?"

"Only to the kind I invite." I flashed him a saccharine smile, and he chuckled.

Connor Morgan was sitting in my apartment, laughing at me like I was the funniest thing he'd ever seen.

"Are you done?"

"I'm going to give it to you straight, El. I want another chance."

"You want another..."

"Chance." Connor stood, sliding his arm around my waist. "Last night was... you blew my fucking mind, El. And I woke up, ready for round two, and you were gone."

"So it's about sex," I huffed.

"Fuck, no. That's not... the sex was amazing. You were amazing. But I meant what I said last night. I've waited a long time for another shot with you."

"I don't understand why you're saying all of this."

He cupped my face, brushing his thumb over my jaw. "Walking away from you is my biggest regret, El. But I was a different guy back then. Selfish. Consumed with the idea of winning. The only thing I wanted back then was to be the best, to make my mark on the team, and I couldn't afford any distractions. And you, kitten, you were the worst kind."

"You hurt me, Connor."

"Fuck, baby, I know. I know." He dipped his head, touching it to mine. "I'm older and wiser now. I know it doesn't have to be a choice between hockey and you. I can have both. I can—"

"Connor." My breath caught at his words. His wild confession. "You don't even know me."

"I know your first coffee of the morning is black with an extra shot. I know you hang out in the romance section a lot in the library. I know that you work out three times a week. Four if you can be bothered. You're always at least two minutes early for class, and you keep your friend circle small. You recently got out of a four-month relationship, but I don't want to talk about that because the idea of you with another guy makes me want to punch something."

"What... how..." My brain couldn't process the overload of information. "Have you been stalking me?"

"I like to call it paying attention." He shrugged, a faint blush washing over his cheeks. "I'd planned to ask you out before the summer break, but you'd just started dating Richard"—his face screwed up—"and I didn't want to get in the way of that."

"Oh my God. All this time you..."

"All this time."

"Connor, I don't know what to say."

"Say yes, El. Give me another shot. We already

know the sex is fire, but I'm pretty confident I can rock your emotional socks too."

Nervous laughter bubbled up inside me. "You did not just say that."

"Oh, I did." His mouth hovered over mine, barely touching. "And I meant every word."

The air crackled, alive with anticipation. My body remembered how good he'd made me feel. And she wanted more. God, she wanted so much more. But I wasn't seriously considering it, was I?

Connor had been watching me for two years. Biding his time. Figuring out when to make his move. I didn't know whether to be mildly freaked out or oddly flattered.

"Don't overthink it," he whispered, his minty breath fanning my face. "I knew that first night that you had the power to ruin me, El. I wasn't prepared to take the risk then, but I am now."

My heart crashed wildly in my chest. He was serious. Deadly serious. And he was looking at me like I held his heart in the palm of my hand.

What was happening right now?

"I... I don't know what to say." The words felt as wrong as they sounded because my heartstrings were tugging me toward saying yes. To throwing caution to the wind and jumping in with both feet.

But it was Connor Morgan.

A Lakers hockey player.

One of the most popular guys on campus.

I liked the quiet, anonymous life. I didn't bloom under the spotlight; I withered.

And yet...

"Say yes, El. Give me a shot, and let me show you how good together we could be."

"Yes."

The word spilled from my lips, surprising us both. But it felt right.

It felt... good.

And when Connor anchored me to him and kissed me, one of his hands on my ass and one buried in my hair, I let him.

Because something had brought us to this moment. Call it kismet or fate or divine intervention. But this guy—this gorgeous man—had broken my heart once.

Maybe it was time to give him a chance to fix it.

EPILOGUE

CONNOR

"Three months, man. Who'd have thought it?" Austin said.

"What can I say?" I wrapped my arm around Ella's waist and drew her into my side. "She's a keeper."

"And you're such a charmer." She grinned up at me, earning us some hoots and hollers from the guys.

Three months in, and they still liked to give me shit about being the first player on the team to get a serious girlfriend. Even Coach Tucker participated sometimes. But he couldn't grumble. My performance on the ice had never been better. Knowing my girl was in the stands, watching me play, and wearing my jersey was like nothing else in the world.

And truthfully, I couldn't wait to see some of these assholes meet the women who would bring them to their fucking knees. Because it would come. In time, it would come, and I'd be right there to give them as much shit as they'd given me over the last few months.

Noah fake retched, flashing Ella a goofy grin.

"You know, Noah, when you finally meet the girl of your dreams, I hope she gives you hell."

"Never going to happen, babe."

"Holden," a low growl rumbled in my chest, "We talked about this. What are the rules?"

Everyone snickered, and Noah ducked his head like a scolded child. "Rule number one," he murmured, "I must not inappropriately touch, kiss, or look at Ella."

"Good," I smirked. "And rule number two?"

"I must never refer to Ella in a sexual way."

"And three?"

"I must refrain from calling Ella, babe, baby, chick, or hot girl."

"Does that about cover it?" I asked Ella, and she fought a smile.

"I think that covers it. Although I quite like it when he called me hot chick."

The guys all exploded with laughter, and I nuzzled Ella's neck. "It's a good thing I love you, *hot chick*."

"Hmm," she twisted her fingers into my jersey. "I love it when you talk dirty to me."

"Oh Jesus," Aiden appeared, glowering at the two of us. "I thought we were watching the game."

"We are." My eyes narrowed. "Why, Dumfries? You got a problem with my girl being here?"

"Con." Ella shook her head.

It wasn't that Aiden didn't like her. He just didn't like the new dynamic between the team since she agreed to be mine. To him, girls were the ultimate distraction—a way to burn off some steam and scratch an itch, nothing more.

"Just thought it was guys' night."

"Give them a break, Dumfries," Kellan said, tipping his beer toward me. "Ella is good people, and one day, it might be your girl coming around to—"

"Nah, nobody is sweet enough to put up with Dumfries' mood swings."

"Fuck off, Linc." The two of them started going at it.

"Hey, you two, knock it off," Kellan boomed.

"Fuck's sake, here we go again. Do you want to get out of here?" I whispered to Ella, and she smiled at me, scraping her nails over my jaw.

"Honestly, there's no place I'd rather be. I love you, Connor, and that includes everything that comes with loving you."

Shit. Emotion swelled in my chest. We'd moved fast, too fast by most people's standards. But when you knew, you knew, and I realized now I'd spent two years falling in love with Ella from afar.

So what was only three months to everyone else felt a whole lot longer for me.

Ella had embraced my life with the team, the crazy that came with being around a bunch of horny goofballs most of the time.

And I loved her all the more for it.

Grabbing the back of her neck, I touched my head to hers, breathing her in.

My girl.

My Ella.

The woman I planned on having a very long and happy future with.

"I love you, baby, so fucking much."

I kissed her, not giving a fuck that we had an audience that included most of the team. They were used to it by now. I couldn't be around Ella without touching her. They didn't get it now. But one day, they would.

One day, love would come around and knock them on their asses too.

And I couldn't wait to watch it happen.

ABOUT THE AUTHOR

Angsty. Edgy. Addictive Romance

USA Today and *Wall Street Journal* bestselling author of over forty mature young adult and new adult novels, L. A. is happiest writing the kind of books she loves to read: addictive stories full of teenage angst, tension, twists and turns.

Home is a small town in the middle of England where she currently juggles being a full-time writer with being a mother/referee to two little people. In her spare time (and when she's not camped out in front of the laptop) you'll most likely find L. A. immersed in a book, escaping the chaos that is life.

L. A. loves connecting with readers.

The best places to find her are:
www.lacotton.com

Printed in Great Britain
by Amazon